A Little Princess

Adapted by M.J. Carr
From the screenplay by
Richard LaGravenese and Elizabeth Chandler
Based on the book by Frances Hodgson Burnett

SCHOLASTIC INC.
New York Toronto London Auckland Sydney

WARNER BROS. PRESENTS
A MARK JOHNSON/BALTIMORE PICTURES PRODUCTION AN ALFONSO CUARÓN FILM "A LITTLE PRINCESS"
ELEANOR BRON LIAM CUNNINGHAM AND INTRODUCING LIESEL MATTHEWS MUSIC BY PATRICK DOYLE EXECUTIVE PRODUCERS ALAN C. BLOMQUIST AND AMY EPHRON
SCREENPLAY BY RICHARD LaGRAVENESE AND ELIZABETH CHANDLER BASED ON THE NOVEL BY FRANCES HODGSON BURNETT
PRODUCED BY MARK JOHNSON DIRECTED BY ALFONSO CUARÓN

G GENERAL AUDIENCES
All Ages Admitted

ISBN 0-590-48627-6

12 11 10 9 8 7 6 5 4 3 2 1   5 6 7 8 9/9 0/0

Printed in the U.S.A.   37

First Scholastic printing, June 1995

*I*ndia is an old land, rich in beauty. Wizened elephants bathe in the rivers. The mountains that tower above the land are among the tallest of all on earth. Though Sara Crewe was British, she grew up in India. Her father was a captain in the army and had been stationed there since before Sara was born. India was the only home she knew.

Sara loved the wild, tangled countryside. She played in the river with her friend Laki. She listened to the stories that Laki's mother told. The stories were Indian legends about a princess named Sita and a prince named Rama. Sara begged to hear the stories again and again.

"Have you ever known a real princess?" she asked.

Laki's mother smiled a knowing smile. "All women are princesses," she replied.

When Sara was ten, war broke out. Her father received orders to take his regiment to the front. Because Sara's mother had died when Sara was quite young, there would be no one to take care of her. Captain Crewe knew that he must send his young daughter off to school.

"But why must I go all the way to America?" Sara asked.

"You'll be going to the same school your mother went to," her father told her. "In a city called New York."

Sara and her father set off on the long journey. As they waited on the dock, Sara looked at the crowds that thronged the seaport. Her eye rested on a man in a turban. A monkey sat chattering on the man's shoulders. Sara grasped her father's hand tightly. She knew she would be leaving everything that she loved.

"I'll spend every moment with you until we get to New York," her father tried to reassure her. They boarded the ship. It pulled from the dock and sailed toward the dark, vast ocean. "You'll always be my little princess," he said.

That night, bright stars spattered the sky. Sara and her father took a stroll on the deck of the ship. Her father clutched something in his hand. It was gold and glittering.

"I want you to have this," he said. In his palm he held a locket. "I gave it to your mother on her wedding day."

Sara opened the locket. Inside were two photos, one of Captain Crewe and the other of her mother.

"She was so beautiful!" exclaimed Sara.

Music drifted on to the deck from the ship's ballroom.

"She used to love to dance," remembered Captain Crewe. He took Sara's hands. Together, he and Sara waltzed around the empty, moonlit deck.

All too soon the ship arrived in New York. The city was abustle with carriages. Buildings rose up everywhere. Sara and her father arrived at the school and climbed the steps to the entrance. A plump, cheerful woman answered the door. It was Amelia Minchin.

"Hello!" she exclaimed heartily. "You must be Captain Crewe! My, my," she grinned, "you *do* look rich!"

"Amelia!" another voice interrupted. It was Miss
Minchin, Amelia's sister, the director of Miss
Minchin's Seminary for Girls. Miss Minchin's face
was sour and pinched, not at all cheerful like
Amelia's. "Follow me," she said sternly. Miss Minchin
led Sara and her father on a tour of the school.

"We have rules governing behavior," she began
her lecture. "The first is the Communication Rule.
Except during free time, no girl may communicate
with another, either by word, look, or manner."

Miss Minchin led Sara and her father into the classroom. As Sara watched, one of the girls, Lavinia, grabbed the pigtail of another and dipped it into her inkwell. When she saw Sara watching, she sneered. Sara was not at all sure she was going to like Lavinia. She wasn't sure she was going to like the school, either.

Miss Minchin's tour ended at Sara's bedroom.
The room was decorated prettily, and had been filled
with books and toys.

"No expense is to be spared on my daughter,"
Captain Crewe instructed Miss Minchin. "My solicitor
will send you a check every month."

"Of course," sniffed Miss Minchin. She left Sara
and her father alone to say their good-byes.

In the room was a doll named Emily. "Whenever you get afraid," Sara's father told her, "or if you miss me terribly, just tell Emily. She'll get the message to me and I'll send one back right away. When you hug Emily, you'll really be getting a hug from me."

"Really?" asked Sara.

"Magic works if you believe in it," said her father. "That's the way it becomes real."

He walked down the stairs and stepped into the carriage that awaited him.

"Good-bye, Princess," he called up to Sara.

Now that Sara was on her own, it took her a while to make friends. Lavinia played one mean prank on her after another. One day, when the girls were exercising outside in the yard, Lavinia pushed Sara headfirst into Amelia. Another time, she snuck upstairs into Sara's room and tore her things from the shelves and closets, leaving the room in a shambles.

Little by little, though, Sara did make friends. One day, she heard someone crying. It was Lottie, one of the youngest girls in the school.

"I want my mama!" Lottie sobbed.

"You'll see her soon," Sara said to comfort her.

Lottie wailed harder. "No I won't! She's dead! I'll never see her again!"

"I don't have a mother, either," Sara said gently. "She's in Heaven. She has wings of silk and a crown of golden roses."

Lottie stopped crying. Her eyes opened wide.

"Your mama's an angel, too," Sara continued. "The angels live in a gleaming white castle, surrounded by hundreds of flowers."

Sara's story was so beautiful, it attracted another listener as well. Becky, a young servant girl, leaned over the banister to listen. Sara turned to say hello, but Becky fled up the stairs.

Sara chased after Becky. She found her at the top of a long staircase in a small attic bedroom. Becky was rubbing her sore, swollen feet with a piece of ice. When she saw Sara, she jumped up.

"Begging your pardon, miss," she said, "but I'm not allowed to talk to the girls in the school. If you stay up here, we'll both be in trouble."

Sara didn't want to get Becky in trouble. She said good-bye and made her way back down the stairs. She liked Becky, though. She hoped they would find a way to be friends.

One Sunday was Visitors Day. Sara helped her friend Ermengarde tie a festive ribbon in her hair. She watched from the stairway as Ermengarde and the other girls raced down to the parlor to greet their mothers and fathers. The families seemed so happy, chatting and laughing. Sara missed her own father. She fingered the locket he had given her.

That night, Sara wrote her father. "Today was Visitors Day. I wish you could have been here. I hugged Emily extra hard just to make sure you got the message. Please don't get hurt in the war. And please remember every day how much I love you."

Far away, in the front lines of the war, Captain Crewe crouched in a trench. The roar of enemy planes drew near. When Captain Crewe received orders to retreat, he started to make his way down the long, narrow tunnel of the trench. Suddenly, he noticed a young, wounded soldier lying at his feet. As enemy planes flew overhead, he hoisted the young man over his shoulder and tried to carry him. But before Captain Crewe could make his escape, the planes swooped down and sprayed the area with poison gas. Captain Crewe began to cough and choke. He and the young soldier fell unconscious.

Back at the school, Miss Minchin and the girls were celebrating Sara's birthday. Everyone crowded around as Sara cut her cake.

Just then, the doorbell rang. Captain Crewe's solicitor had come, bearing very bad news. He informed Miss Minchin that Captain Crewe had been reported dead. "There will be no more checks for Sara," he said solemnly. "The war left Captain Crewe bankrupt."

Miss Minchin paled. She stormed back to the party to put an end to the festivities. "Your father is dead," she told Sara icily. "And you are left penniless. From now on, you must earn your room and board here. You will move to the attic with Becky and work in the school as a servant."

Miss Minchin marched Sara up to the attic. She deposited her in a tiny, dark bedroom next to Becky's. Cobwebs draped the corners. Rain dripped into dirty puddles from a broken skylight in the low, slanting ceiling. Miss Minchin spied Sara's locket, the one her father had given her. She grabbed it out of Sara's hands. "All your things are mine now," she said. "Report to the kitchen for work tomorrow morning promptly at 5 A.M. Remember, Sara Crewe, you're not a 'princess' any longer."

When Miss Minchin left, Sara sank onto the bed. Her dear father, whom she loved and missed terribly, was dead. Sara was now alone in the world. "Papa," she sobbed. "Oh, Papa . . ."

From that day on, Sara's life was quite different than it had been before. She served the other girls their breakfast. She washed the dishes and mopped the floors. The cook sent Sara on errands, often on the dampest, bleakest days.

One day, a sharp wind blew Sara's shawl off her shoulders. Sara chased it. It fell at the feet of an Indian man named Ram Dass. It was the man in the turban whom Sara had seen on the dock! Before Sara got a chance to speak, she was startled by a cry.

Mr. Randolph, the man who lived next to the school, held a telegram in his shaking hands. The telegram had been delivered by soldiers, who stood by at attention. "Not my son!" Mr. Randolph sobbed. "Please, God, not John!" Ram Dass put his hand on the man's shoulder to comfort him. Sara knew that Mr. Randolph's son had probably been killed in the war, as her father had been.

One chill, autumn night, as Sara trudged back from her errands, a well-dressed boy stopped and pressed a coin in her hand.

I guess I look like a beggar, thought Sara.

Sara took the coin into a bakery and bought a warm, steaming bun to fill her empty stomach. When she came out, she passed a poor woman selling roses. The woman had a baby in her arms. Surely, thought Sara, they need food more than I do. Sara handed the bun to the woman. The woman held out a rose to Sara in return.

"For the princess," the woman said gratefully.

But Sara no longer felt much like a princess at all.

Each night, in the attic, Becky tried to cheer up Sara.

"Don't you want to tell your stories anymore?" she asked. "They might make you feel better."

Sara shook her head. "Stories are just make-believe," she said. "There is no magic."

"Tell me about India," urged Becky.

"India . . ." remembered Sara. "The air smells like spices. Tigers sleep under the trees. Elephants cool themselves in the lakes. . . ."

Becky was right. Sara did feel better when she was telling stories. She tried to remember what her father had told her: "Magic works when you believe in it."

Now that Sara was a servant, Lavinia tormented her more than ever. One day, as Sara reported to Lavinia's room to load her fireplace with coal, Lavinia sniffed rudely.

"What's that smell?" she taunted. "Haven't you had a bath?"

Sara had had enough of Lavinia's smug, snooty ways. She dropped the coal bin and started dancing wildly around. She chanted nonsense words, making them up as she went along.

"What are you doing?" hissed Lavinia.

Sara picked up the coal bin. "I put a curse on you," she said. "A little something I learned from a witch in India." Sara smiled slyly as she left Lavinia gaping in the room.

Sara's friends in the school, though, missed her terribly. Miss Minchin no longer allowed them to talk to her. They saw her only when she served them breakfast or when they passed her mopping the halls. Ermengarde called her friends together. "Sara must feel terrible," she said. "What can we do?" She looked around at the other girls.

"I know!" she declared at last. "We'll get her locket back!"

The girls slipped downstairs into Miss Minchin's office. They knew Sara's locket must be in the office somewhere. Ermengarde pulled open a drawer.

"I got it!" she cried.

Just then, Miss Minchin came back from her errands. Becky had been keeping watch. She cried out to distract Miss Minchin while the others snuck out of the office. The girls scattered to their rooms. Sara would be so surprised!

Sara was outside, sweeping the steps of the school. She noticed Ram Dass and Mr. Randolph getting into a carriage. Sara heard Mr. Randolph tell the driver to go to the hospital. She heard him say that there was a wounded soldier who might be his son.

When the carriage returned, it brought the soldier home. The soldier's eyes were bandaged. He had lost all memory after the trauma of the war. The soldier, though, was not Mr. Randolph's son.

"He may not be your son," Ram Dass suggested kindly, "but he's sick and has nowhere to go. He needs us to care for him."

Sara saw the carriage pass, though she didn't see the face of the soldier inside. She didn't know that that soldier — wounded, feeble, and suffering from amnesia — was her father.

That night, the girls crept up the stairs to the attic. Ermengarde led the way.

"Princess Sara," she announced, "we'd like to present you with something."

Lottie stepped forward. She held out the golden locket and laid it in Sara's palm.

"I don't know what to say," Sara stammered. "You're the best friends anyone could ask for."

The girls settled around Sara and begged her for a story. Sara began to tell the story she remembered from India about Princess Sita and Prince Rama. Just at that moment, the skylight banged open. In jumped Hanuman, the monkey who lived across the alley with Ram Dass. The girls squealed in delight.

The girls' shrieks attracted the attention of Miss Minchin. She climbed out of bed and tore up the stairs to the attic.

"What's going on here?" she demanded.

Miss Minchin sent the students back downstairs. She ordered Becky to return to her room.

"As for you, Sara Crewe, it's time you learned that real life has nothing to do with your little fantasies and dreams. It's a cruel, nasty world out there. Do you understand what I'm saying?"

"I understand it," said Sara, "but I don't believe in it."

"Don't tell me you still fancy yourself a princess," Miss Minchin sneered. "Look around you, child. Better yet, look in a mirror."

Sara gathered herself to her full height. She answered Miss Minchin with all the authority she could muster. "I *am* a princess," she said. "All girls are. Even if they live in tiny old attics. Even if they dress in rags. Didn't your father ever tell you that?"

Sara's courage angered Miss Minchin even more.

"You'll go without food all day tomorrow," she sputtered. "And Becky as well!" With that, she turned on her heel and stormed out of the room.

When she had gone, Becky snuck back into Sara's room to comfort her.

"What will we do without food?" she asked.

"We'll make a feast of our own tonight," declared Sara. "We'll make-believe it. Like magic. Look. There on the table. I see a platter loaded with sausages. And next to it?"

"A tray of steaming-hot muffins!" chimed in Becky.

Together, the two girls imagined a richly set table. They imagined that they themselves were dressed in silks and finery. It almost took their hunger and misery away.

Across the alley, Ram Dass listened from his window. He was touched by the courage of the two hapless girls. He pet Hanuman, his monkey, and wondered how he might help.

The next morning, Becky and Sara awoke side by side. Hanuman hopped about between them. Sara sat up. Covering the bed was an exquisite silk quilt. Across the room, a crackling fire had been lit in the grate, which was usually cold.

Sara couldn't believe her eyes. The floor was now covered with a rich, plush rug. Two armchairs straddled a small table. The table was set with trays of food!

Sara walked hesitantly to the table and lifted the cover of one of the trays. It was filled with sausages!

"Look, Becky!" she cried. "Just what we ordered!"

The two hungry girls fell upon the food and gobbled it up gleefully.

Across the alley, Ram Dass smiled. He fed breakfast
to his own guest, Captain Crewe.

"A muffin, Sahib," he offered.

"Sahib . . . " murmured Captain Crewe.

"It's an Indian word," said Ram Dass. "Do you
know it?"

"Everything is a blur," the Captain said, shaking
his head. "I wish I could sort it out."

"You'll remember," Ram Dass assured him.

That day, Sara worked from dawn till dusk. Though the work was hard, it seemed lighter since she had been well-fed. At the end of the day, she climbed to her room. There were the rug and the trays from the food. It hadn't been a dream, after all.

Just then, in her office, Miss Minchin discovered the locket was missing. She stalked up the stairs to the attic.

"Where's the locket?" she demanded.

Miss Minchin gasped when she saw Sara's room. Where did Sara get the rug? And the silk quilt and trays of food? "Why, you're nothing but a thief!" she accused Sara. "You stole all of this! Just like you stole the locket! I'm calling the police!"

Miss Minchin locked Sara in her room. She marched down the stairs to make the call. "I want you to pick up the girl immediately!" she demanded.

Sara knew that she must escape. Becky helped her carry a plank to the window. They set one edge on Sara's windowsill and rested the other across the alley, on Ram Dass's window. As they worked, a driving rain began pelting the rooftop. Sara saw the police wagon pull up in front of the school. She clambered out the window and edged across the plank.

"I'll come back for you," she promised Becky.

Miss Minchin led the policemen up the stairs.

Before Sara reached the opposite window, the plank slipped and clattered down three stories into the alley below. Sara grabbed on to the ledge of Ram Dass's window. She pulled herself into his room.

"Don't just stand there!" Miss Minchin commanded the police. "Go next door! Find her!"

As Sara stole down the stairs of the quiet old house, Miss Minchin banged on the front door.

"Open up!" she cried. "There's a child hiding in this house unlawfully!"

The policemen poured into the house and scattered to search for Sara. One opened the door to the parlor where Sara was hiding. Just then, lightning flashed. The lights went out! Sara slipped into the study next door. She collapsed against the door and began to cry. She did not know that her father was sitting in the room.

"Why are you crying?" he asked. He stepped into the light of the fire. Sara saw his face.

"Papa!" she gasped.

"Do you know me?" he asked.

The doors to the study swung open. Miss Minchin burst in with the police.

"Papa," Sara pleaded. "Don't you remember me? Tell them!"

But Captain Crewe could not remember anything, even his daughter. The police grabbed Sara by the wrists. Frantically, she began to call out.

"Remember India? And Emily? Remember the locket?" Sara sobbed as the police dragged her out the door.

Suddenly, Captain Crewe's memory was jogged. "Sara!" he shouted. He ran to the street. Sara broke free and raced to his arms.

"Papa," she cried. "Oh, Papa, you're back!"

Once Captain Crewe was well, he made plans to return to India with Sara.

Mr. Randolph was waiting for them outside the school.

"I can't thank you enough," Captain Crewe told him.

Mr. Randolph smiled warmly. "It was no more than what you tried to do for my son," he replied.

Sara and her father arranged to take Becky with them. Captain Crewe brought the two girls to say good-bye to their friends.

As a farewell present, Sara gave her school friends her doll, Emily. "When you hug her, you'll really be getting a hug from me," she told them.

"Then we'll hug her every day!" cried Ermengarde.

Some weeks later, Sara, Captain Crewe, and Becky stood on the deck of a grand ocean liner sailing toward India. The glorious, tropical countryside stretched out in front of them along the horizon. Sara looked out on the land. So much had happened since they had left. Now, never again would she go hungry. Never again would she be wrested from her father and those she loved. Lush, hot India beckoned. It welcomed the travelers home with open arms.